This edition first published in Great Britain in 1995, reprinted in 1997
and 1998 by Macdonald Young Books.

This edition published in 2001 by Hodder Wayland,
an imprint of Hodder Children's Books

© Hodder Wayland 2001

Hodder Children's Books
A division of Hodder Headline Ltd
338 Euston Road, London NW1 3BH

Photoset in 16/24 Meridien

Printed and bound in Belgium by Proost N.V.

British Library Cataloguing in Publications Data available

ISBN: 07500 17147

Rob Childs
Guy Fawkes and the Gunpowder Gang

Illustrated by Gini Wade

HODDER
Wayland

an imprint of Hodder Children's Books

1
Remember, Remember!

Guy Fawkes stared up at the waiting
hangman. He shivered, but not with
fear. The cold January wind cut through
his thin clothes.

He caught the eye of his close friend,
Thomas Winter.

"Be brave, Tom!" he cried over the
noise of the crowd.

"Farewell!" came the reply. "Till we
meet again in a better place."

A guard told them to be silent. "It
will be Hell, not Heaven, where traitors
like you are going this day," he sneered.

Guy shook his head. He could think of so many better places to be. His mind roamed back to happier times as a boy, running free in the beautiful green dales of the county of Yorkshire. And even to the city of York itself where he was born in 1570, thirty-five summers ago.

He remembered the rough and
tumbles he had enjoyed at school there
with Jack and Kit Wright. Always up to
some mischief, the boys' laughing faces
swam before him. They were both dead
now. Killed after the failure of the
Gunpowder Plot – surely the greatest
piece of mischief ever planned.

Memories returned, too, of the years spent in the dales village of Scotton and the visit once to nearby Knaresborough with Tom. They had gone to see the cave where its famous witch, Mother Shipton, used to live.

"Dare you to go in," Tom had grinned at him.

"I will, if you will," he'd whispered back.

Later, outside the cave, they had shared the same secret wish at the magic well. The two boys dipped their hands together into the pool of cold water in the rock. "I wish to become a soldier," he'd repeated after Tom, "and help to make England a Catholic country once again."

Now Guy watched sadly as Tom was pushed towards the scaffold by the guards. "It seems always to have been like this with us," he sighed. "Young Tom leading the way and me following."

The crowd roared loudly. "God save the King! Long live the King!"

Then they began a popular, mocking chant to taunt all the men about to die.

"Remember, remember,
The Fifth of November,
Gunpowder, Treason and Plot.
We see no reason,
Why Gunpowder Treason,
Should ever be forgot!"

Guy could hardly believe it was really happening to him. The whole thing was like some terrible nightmare. "How did I get myself into this mess?" he wondered bitterly. "How did it all start...?"

2
Keep it Secret

Late one damp, spring evening in 1604, as Guy was gazing miserably into the dying embers of his camp fire, he received a surprise visit from an old friend. Like Guy, Tom Winter had been fighting abroad in Europe for many years, so they had rarely had chance to meet.

"I'm homesick, Tom, and tired of war," Guy confessed. "I wish sometimes that I had never become a soldier."

At first it had all seemed like a great adventure to Guy when he joined the Catholic Spanish army to seek his fame and fortune. But things had not worked out for him as well as he'd expected and now he wanted to leave.

"Why not come back to England with me, Guido?" said Tom, using the Spanish form of Guy's name. "We have need of your skills and courage."

"Who has need of me?" Guy asked with interest.

"The Catholics of England. Since King James came to the throne last year, he has broken his promises to allow us to worship in our own way. He has begun to pass cruel laws against our Faith."

"But what can I do to help?"

Tom checked that no-one else was listening. "Remember the second part of our boyhood wish?" he said in a hushed voice. Guy nodded eagerly. "Well, there is now a group of people in England who are wanting to make it all come true..."

Guy decided to return and found
himself one night in a locked upstairs
room of a London inn with four other
men. Three of them he knew well from
days of old – Tom, of course, Jack Wright
and Thomas Percy, once a neighbour at
Scotton. The fourth, a tall, handsome
man, did most of the talking.

"Swear a sacred oath on the Holy Bible," Robert Catesby urged them, "to keep secret everything I am about to tell you."

"I swear," Guy promised, resting his hand on the Bible.

The others did the same and Catesby explained his plans.

"We are going to blow up the House of Lords with gunpowder!" he began, looking each man, in turn, in the eye to win their trust. "As King James makes his speech to Parliament, he and all his Protestant supporters will be killed."

"What will happen after that?" Guy asked, wide-eyed.

"We shall have an armed force ready to ride upon London," Catesby answered, his face alight. "The victory will be ours and soon there will again be a Catholic monarch on the English throne."

Guy gulped and ran his hand through his neat, reddish-brown beard. He knew there was no turning back now. He must do what must be done – or die in the attempt.

"Aagh, my aching back!" Tom groaned. "This heavy digging will be the death of me."

In the flickering shadows of their lanterns, Guy stared down at his own blistered and bleeding hands. "Nay, Tom, it will bring about the death of King James! Keep going – we are doing the work of God."

"But this tunnel is still so short and we have been scraping at stone for weeks," Tom sighed. "I fear the wall is too thick."

Percy had rented a house next door to Parliament and the plotters were trying to dig a tunnel between the two buildings to smuggle in all the gunpowder. It was a difficult task for so few men to carry out, especially when the narrow tunnel kept filling with water.

By early 1605, despite more Catholics joining the gang, little progress had been made. Guy prayed to God for some sign of fresh hope and suddenly it seemed that his prayers had been answered.

They would not need the tunnel after all; a storeroom had become vacant in the cellars below the House of Lords – right underneath the King's throne!

3
Bomb Warning!

The choppy waters of the River Thames lapped up the stone steps leading to the Parliament buildings.

"Steady! Be careful!" hissed Robert Catesby into the darkness.

Kit Wright grinned. "Do not worry. We will not let the gunpowder get wet!"

He helped his elder brother, Jack, lift another barrel of gunpowder from the rocking boat. Together, they staggered under its weight along the alleyway towards the cellars.

"Good, now put it over there with the others," said Guy, holding up his lantern to guide them. He was in charge of the cellar store because of all his experience with gunpowder in the Spanish army.

Boatload after boatload of gunpowder was rowed across the river that night until thirty-six barrels were stacked in the cellar. Guy made sure they were completely hidden by mounds of coal and firewood.

"You have done well, my friend," Catesby praised him. "And you deserve the honour yourself of lighting the fuse to set off the huge explosion. Your name will go down in history!"

Guy laughed. "People will only remember me if I am stupid enough to blow myself up as well!"

"You have plenty of time to practise getting it right," Jack Wright reminded him. "King James has postponed the opening of Parliament again until his so-called 'lucky' day – Tuesday, the fifth of November!"

During the months of preparations that followed, Catesby persuaded a number of wealthy Catholics to enter the Plot too. They promised to provide money, horses, armour and weapons to make certain of its success after the King was dead.

The same awful fear haunted everyone, however. Despite the oath of secrecy, the more people that knew of the Plot, the greater the risk that it might be given away – accidentally or on purpose. And one Saturday in late October, it happened.

A letter was sent, unsigned, to Lord
Monteagle, a Catholic friend of several
of the plotters. It warned him not to go
to the opening ceremony. As his servant
read the letter aloud to him, Monteagle
pricked up his ears. "...they shall receive
a terrible blow, this Parliament, and yet
they will not see who hurts them..."

Monteagle did not fully understand what the message meant. But he rode on horseback that very night to show it to the Government's chief ministers.

When Catesby himself heard about the warning, he refused to scrap his plans. "We have gone too far now to stop," he decided. "Let us hope that the Government may think this strange, anonymous letter is merely a hoax."

Nobody knew for certain who had written it, but the main suspicion fell upon Francis Tresham. He was the thirteenth and final member of the gang, and was also Lord Monteagle's brother-in-law.

"I am not to blame for that letter," Tresham kept insisting, but Guy and many of the other plotters did not believe him. Although the danger was now greater, Guy – like the brave soldier he was – still carried out Catesby's orders and continued to guard the cellar alone.

At midnight on the fourth of November, the Government suddenly struck. Troops searched the cellars, the gunpowder was discovered and a man was found with a fuse and matches in the pockets of his cloak.

Guy had been caught red-handed…

4
I am not Afraid to Die

"Who are you?"

"John Johnson," Guy replied, not
wishing to give his real name. Nor
would he say anything about the other
plotters. He knew they would soon learn
of his arrest. Now that the Plot had
failed, he wanted to allow his friends
enough time to escape.

Guy was taken by boat along the Thames to the Tower of London and slung into a tiny, dark cell called Little Ease. He could not either stand up or lie down. "I am sorry for what I tried to do," he told one of the guards, "for I see now that God did not agree with it."

Over the next few days, however, Guy was shown no mercy. When he would not answer any questions, information was slowly forced out of him by torture. His body was stretched and broken on the rack, the most feared instrument of torture in the Tower.

Finally he could stand the terrible
pain no longer and confessed everything
he knew about the Plot. He was almost
too weak by now even to be able to sign
his own name. He managed only a very
shaky and scribbled *Guido* before the
quill pen fell from his trembling hand.

His courage had been wasted.
Unknown to Guy, the Government had
already hunted down the other members
of the gang. After a chase across several
counties, they had all been captured or
killed during a shoot-out at Holbeach
House in Staffordshire.

Guy wept when he heard the news.
Four of them had been shot dead –
Catesby their leader, Percy and both the
Wright brothers. Even Tom was
wounded and joined Guy in the Tower,
along with the other survivors. But
nobody shed any tears for Tresham
when he died in his cell from poison.

At their trial, they were quickly
found guilty of High Treason for plotting
to kill the King. "You will be hung,
drawn and quartered!" announced the
judge. "This is the reward due to
traitors!"

On the actual night of the fifth of
November, the people of London had
celebrated the failure of the Gunpowder
Plot. They lit bonfires and threw straw
figures of Guy Fawkes into the flames to

see him burn. Now, on the last day of
January, 1606, the crowd were
screaming for his blood.

Guy turned pale. He was being saved
until last, but he could not bear to
watch. He looked away towards the
House of Lords, the very building they
had hoped to destroy.

It was too late for any more hopes
and dreams. This was the end.

Guy heard Tom mounting the
hangman's scaffold and wondered if he
was thinking about his elder brother.
Robert Winter had been among the first
group of four plotters executed the day
before.

"I die a true Catholic," Tom cried out to the jeering crowd.

Jeers turned to cheers as he swung on the rope and was then carried off to the axeman's block. And the excitement grew as the next two men met the same fate. Here came the moment they had all been waiting for.

After his torture, Guy needed help to climb the steps of the ladder up to the scaffold. Once there, he knelt in full view of the crowd and made the sign of the cross. "I ask the King and God for forgiveness," he prayed aloud. "I am not afraid to die."

The life of Guy Fawkes was over – but his fame would live on for ever and ever!